THE SAND CASTLE CONTEST

To Matthew Luttmann,
Guelph, Ontario
–R.M.

Text copyright © 2005 by Bob Munsch Enterprises, Ltd.
Illustrations copyright © 2005 by Michael Martchenko.
All rights reserved. Published by Scholastic Inc.
SCHOLASTIC, CARTWHEEL BOOKS, and associated logos
are trademarks and/or registered trademarks of Scholastic Inc.

Library of Congress Cataloging-in-Publication Data Available

ISBN 0-439-74865-8

26 25 24 23   11 12/0

Printed in the U.S.A.   40
First printing, May 2005

THE
SAND CASTLE
CONTEST

by **Robert Munsch**
Illustrated by **Michael Martchenko**

Cartwheel
B·O·O·K·S ®

SCHOLASTIC INC.

New York Toronto London Auckland Sydney
Mexico City New Delhi Hong Kong Buenos Aires

Matthew's father stood in the driveway and said, "I think we are all ready to go! Let's make sure everything is here. Do we have the bicycles?"

"YES!"

"Do we have the food?"

"YES!"

"Do we have the boat?"

"YES!"

"Do we have everything?"

"NO!" yelled Matthew.

"No?" said his dad.

"No!" said Matthew. "We don't have a dog."

"Dog?" said his dad. "We don't even OWN a dog!"

"I know," said Matthew. "Now would be a good time to get a dog."

"No dog!" said his dad. "Now, do we have everything?"

"No!" yelled Matthew. "We don't have my sandbox."

"Matthew," said his mom, "we can't bring the sandbox, but the first place we camp will have a nice beach, and you will have lots of sand to play with."

"Well," said Matthew, "okay."

So they drove and drove and drove and drove and drove, until they came to a place to camp.

Matthew jumped out of the van and ran to the beach.

He came to a girl making a small sand castle and a big sand dog.

She said, "Hi! My name is Kalita and I'm going to win the sand castle contest!"

"WOW!" said Matthew. "I am going to build a sand castle, too. What can I win?"

"You can win a bathtub full of ice cream," said Kalita.

"All right!" said Matthew.

So Matthew made a house with doors and windows and a roof.
He dug out the inside of the house so it had rooms
just like a real house. He made sand tables and
chairs and beds and a TV that had a
sand show on it.

When Matthew was almost done, Kalita came over to look at his house. She had her sand dog on a leash.

"Nice sand house," said Kalita.

"Really, *really* nice sand dog," said Matthew.

A judge came by and said, "Get this house out of here!

Who put this house on the beach?"

"This is my sand house," said Matthew.

"I made it for the sand contest."

"Ha!" said the judge. "I know a real house

when I see one,

and there are

no real houses

allowed on the beach!"

Then he went inside and sat in a sand chair and watched a sand show on TV.

Another judge came by and said, "Get this house out of here! Who put this house on the beach?"

"This is my sand house," said Matthew. "I made it for the sand contest."

"HA!" said the judge. "I know a real house when I see one, and there are no real houses allowed on the beach!"

She went into the bedroom and looked at the sand bed.

She went into the kitchen, opened the refrigerator, and looked at the sand apples and the sand celery and the sand cartons of milk. Then she said, "Little boy, you've got to get this house off the beach."

"This is my sand house," said Matthew, "and I am going to prove it."

"HA!" said the judges.

So Matthew went outside and kicked the sand house right beside the door. It all turned back into an enormous pile of sand and fell on the judges.

"HELP!" yelled the judges, and everyone came running and dug them out.

When the judges were finally out from under the sand, they yelled, "Matthew wins! His sand house was so good that we thought it was a real house."

"Matthew WINS!" everyone yelled, and they gave him a bathtub full of ice cream.

Matthew started eating the ice cream, and he said to Kalita, "Want to help me eat this?"

"Yes," said Kalita.

While they were eating the ice cream, Matthew said, "How come you didn't tell everybody that your dog is sand? I bet you would have won with a sand dog."

"Well," said Kalita, "this is Sandy, my sand dog, and I am going to take him camping and feed him ice cream every day and he is going to be my pet and I am never going to turn him back to sand."

"WOW!" said Matthew. "I wish I had thought of that. Can you show me how to make one?"

"No problem," said Kalita.

And Matthew's mom and dad were so happy with Matthew's amazing sand dog that . . .

they decided to take it camping.